LITTLE
APPALOOSA

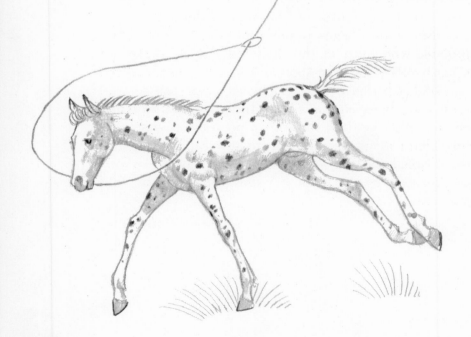

FOREWORD

The first settlers who came to the new world discovered by Christopher Columbus were Spaniards. When they crossed the ocean to their new home, they brought their horses with them. Some of these horses were strikingly marked. Many had black, brown, or auburn dots on white or cream-colored coats. Others had solid-colored foreparts, but their hips were white flecked with spots. These horses, whose ancestry could be traced back to the ancient kingdoms of Asia, were known in the Old World as "les milles fleurs," or horses of a thousand flowers.

The horse, a new animal to the Americas, multiplied and in time spread northward, through Mexico, to the great plains of the Far West. The nomadic Indians of the plains obtained some of these horses. They no longer had to walk but could move swiftly as they followed the great herds of buffalo, their principal source of food and clothing.

By the time the white settlers began to move into the western plains, the Nez Perce Indians, who lived in the sheltered Palouse Valley of Idaho, had large herds of horses. The spotted horse, because of speed and endurance, was highly prized by the Indians as a war pony.

When the many wars between the plains Indians and the white settlers came to an end, great herds of the Indian ponies were destroyed to keep the Indians from leaving the government reservations. Some of their spotted horses escaped and ran wild on the plains. These survivors became known as "horses from the Palouse Valley." This in time was shortened to "appaloosas."

THE AUTHORS

Little
APPALOOSA
by Berta and Elmer Hader

The Macmillan Company, New York

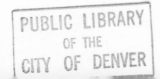

The Macmillan Company, New York
Collier-Macmillan Canada, Ltd., Toronto, Ontario
Printed in the United States of America
Seventh Printing, 1967

jH115Li

Little Appaloosa

is affectionately dedicated to
Lee Harold and his horse "Pal."

"JIMINY CRICKET!" Little Ben stared at the colt running beside the big black horse his father was riding. The dust, raised as they trotted past the house, made the Wind River Mountains at the far edge of the grassy range, disappear from view for an instant. Ben rubbed the dust from his eyes and looked again. Then he dashed from the ranch house porch to the corral.

"Hey, Dad," he shouted. "What kind of a colt is that? Where did you get him?"

Ben's father smiled as he lifted the saddle from his horse's back. He looked at the little spotted colt standing close by.

"He is an Indian pony," he said. "A little appaloosa. The Indians used to raise a lot of them. They are hard to find now. I bought him for your birthday from Chief Lone Eagle over at the Wind River Reservation. His mother died and we'll have to raise him on a bottle. When he is big enough and you have trained him to be a good cow pony, you can come with me on the round-ups." He took the bridle off his horse and turned him loose. The little appaloosa followed the big black horse across the corral.

Little Ben loved horses. He was a born rider. He had been in the saddle ever since he was a baby. He looked with shining eyes at HIS colt—his very own.

"Gosh, Dad," was all he could say. He turned and ran as fast as he could to the ranch house.

"Mom," he called. "Come on out and see my birthday present. It's a surprise. Hurry, Mom."

Little Ben's mother came out of the kitchen and followed him to the corral.

"Look, Mom," said little Ben. "He's a uh-uh, a appaloosa. I've never seen a colt spotted like that before. Have you?"

"No, son. I never have. Isn't he pretty?" She smiled as the colt lifted his head and whinnied a greeting from the far side of the corral. "Be gentle with him, son," she said, "And he will be your friend." She looked toward the barn. "Call your father now. Your supper is on the table." She walked back to the house.

After supper, Ben warmed some milk and filled a pan with a bran mash. The colt was hungry. He quickly finished the bottle of milk and licked the pan of mash clean.

Before going to sleep that night, Ben slipped out of bed and

tiptoed to the window. The stillness of the moonlit night was broken by the steady chirping of crickets. The spotted pony stood close beside Blackie, his father's best riding horse. Thrilled by the thought that he had a horse of his very own, little Ben went back to bed. The spotted colt was a wonderful birthday present.

Ben was up early the next morning. He warmed some milk on the kitchen stove and filled the colt's bottle. Then he ran over to the corral. His happy whistle rose like the song of a lark in the clear morning air. The spotted colt whinnied softly and met him at the corral gate.

"Jiminy Crickets!" said Ben delightedly. "He KNOWS me!"

It did not take the colt long to empty the bottle of milk. Then
he followed little Ben into the barn. He remembered the pan of
warm mash he had had for supper the night before.

"Bennieeee. Breakfast is ready," his mother called.

Little Ben picked up the feeding pan from the bench and
hurried out of the barn, followed by the eager colt. "Coming,
Mother," he called. At the corral gate he stopped to rub the
colt's pretty head. "I'll bring you some mash, after I've had my
breakfast," he said.

After breakfast, little Ben mixed a pan of bran mash and fed his colt. Then he sat on the corral fence and watched the ranch hands train the horses just brought in from the range. It was dangerous and exciting work. The spotted colt watched, too.

Every day after he had finished helping his mother with the

chores, little Ben hurried to the corral to see his colt. He always spoke gently to him and the little appaloosa soon trusted him as a friend. Before many days had passed Ben put a halter on the colt and led him around the corral. He never forgot to pet the little appaloosa and praise him at the end of the lesson.

When another spring came to the range, the colt was almost as tall as the other ranch horses. He was a yearling now and had learned to nibble at the sweet grasses that grew in the field outside the corral. Ben was taller, too. He looked forward to the day when his colt would be strong enough to ride. He wanted to be a good cowboy and in his spare moments, he practiced throwing the lasso. When he tired of roping a stake in the ground or the corral fence posts, he lassoed Terry, the ranch dog. Sometimes he lassoed Barnaby, the goat. The long summer days passed swiftly by.

The winter on the plains was mild that year. Ben's pony learned from the other horses how to paw the snow off the ground and nibble the grass underneath. His thick winter coat kept him warm. When spring returned to the range and the sun melted the last of the winter's snow, Ben's little appaloosa was a handsome two-year-old.

After the roundup that spring, Ben's father sold some cattle. When he came back from town, he brought a saddle for the young appaloosa. "You'll soon be able to ride your pony, son," he said. "Better get him used to a saddle. You've both got a lot to learn before going out on a roundup."

Ben followed his father's advice. First he let the pony look at the saddle and smell it. Then he put the saddle on his back. Ben kept the saddle on the pony's back a little longer each day until he got used to it. Then he tightened the cinch and led him around the corral. "You're going to be the best cow pony on the range, Pal," said Ben. He patted his pony affectionately and gave him a carrot. The young appaloosa ate the treat Ben gave him and looked for more. He liked carrots. Ben could hardly wait for the time to come when he could ride his pony and go with his father to the roundup.

It was summer before Ben got into the saddle for his first ride. Though the pony was used to the saddle and had been trained to obey the lightest touch of the reins, carrying a rider was a new and strange experience. He backed and circled and pranced around the corral. Ben hoped the little pony wouldn't try to buck him out of the saddle. He remembered the wild rides of the cowboys when they were training the range horses. "Easy, Pal," he said in a gentle voice. "It's only me. No one is going to hurt you." The soft-spoken words of his rider calmed the young horse.

After a few days of riding around the corral, Ben and the spotted pony were traveling happily over the range trails. Each day they went a little further from the house. Ben taught the appaloosa to start, turn, and stop quickly at a signal from him. When they returned to the corral, Ben never forgot to give his pony a piece of carrot or a crust of bread as a reward for a lesson well learned.

"Good work, son," said Ben's father one morning. He had kept a watchful eye on the training of the colt. "Your little appaloosa is a smart one. He is full of spirit and he will make a fine cow pony."

Ben was pleased by his father's words and he was proud of the little spotted pony.

The nearest neighbor was a rancher who lived high up in the foothills. The rancher's wife had been a school teacher. She now had a big family of children, so she started a ranch school and asked Ben to join the class. Every morning Ben rode to school on

his little appaloosa. After school, Ben always took a different path home. No matter which direction he started, the pony could always find his way to the home corral. The pony grew wiser and stronger every day.

Winters come early to the ranges on the high plateaus and sometimes the snow was so deep Ben couldn't ride his appaloosa to school. The ranch horses and cattle grew heavy coats that kept them warm. The spotted pony learned that the barn was a good shelter when cold winds blew down from the mountains or a blizzard swept the range. Winters are long in the mountain country and everyone was glad when spring returned to the ranges, bringing a new growth of wild hay, alfalfa, and sweet smelling sage. Ben rode his horse to the neighbor's school whenever the trails were passable.

One day on the way home from school, a sudden storm swept down from the mountains. It brought a late snow that soon covered the foothills and the plains. All signs of the well-known trails disappeared as the storm turned into a blizzard. Ben buttoned up the collar of his warm woolen jacket. He had never been out in such a storm before and he had lost all sense of direction. He gave the little appaloosa his head. "Home, Pal," he said. "You've got to find the way home. I'm lost." The spotted pony shook his mane and walked steadily through the ever-deepening snow. Ben held on to the pommel of the saddle

with hands stiff with cold. He thought of old Matt the sheep herder, who had been lost in just such a blizzard and had never been seen again and his courage almost left him. Suddenly Pal quickened his pace and soon Ben saw the well-remembered roof of the ranch house. In a few minutes they were inside the warm barn. Blackie whinnied a welcome.

"Good ol' Pal," whispered Ben as he hung the bridle on a peg. "I'm sure glad you found the way home." He brushed the snow and ice off his pony and rubbed him dry. Then he filled the manger with hay, and emptied a big pan of oats in the feed box.

Ben's mother met him at the corral gate. She had been worried about him ever since the beginning of the storm. Ben's father was away on business and she was alone. With a sigh of relief, she hurried Ben into the kitchen for a bowl of hot soup. The storm gathered in fury outside and rattled the ranch house windows. Above the noise of the storm, they heard the howl of a hungry coyote. Safe and warm in the ranch house kitchen, Ben finished a second bowl of hot soup. His experience in the blizzard would not soon be forgotten. "Gosh, Mom," he said. "If it hadn't been for my little appaloosa, I wouldn't be here now. I was lost. Pal found the way home."

Ben's mother was grateful, too. She knew how dangerous it was to be lost in a blizzard on the range.

One rainy day that spring, Molly Antelope, the grand-daughter of Curly Bear, a chief on the nearby Indian Reservation, came to the kitchen door. She was out of breath from running. "Please come," she gasped. "Our wagon overturned in Panther Gully and my grandfather is hurt." She pointed to her leg. "The wagon fell on him here. He says it hurts bad."

"Oh dear," said Ben's mother. "All the men are out on the range. We will have to send for help." She turned to Ben. "Get your pony and ride as fast as you can to the reservation. Ask the Indian agent to send some men right away. Then find Dr. Mathias. He ought to be at the Trading Post today. Ask him to come. Molly can ride with you. She knows the short cut to the reservation. I'll see what I can do for Molly's grandfather until help comes."

Ben ran to the barn. He slipped a bridle on Pal, led him into the corral and leaped on his back without waiting to put on a saddle. Molly jumped from the fence to the pony's back and held fast to Ben. The sure-footed pony raced away to the Reservation.

Luckily the rain had stopped. The morning sun broke through the storm clouds and a lovely rainbow arched down from the snow covered peaks of the distant mountains to the rolling range land. Near the reservation, they met four braves on their way to the Trading Post. Molly spoke rapidly and told them of the accident. The four Indians wheeled their horses and galloped off to help Curly Bear. Ben and Molly Antelope hurried on to the Agency.

Dr. Mathias was in his office and as soon as his fast gray mare was saddled, he followed Ben and Molly Antelope. Jack rabbits leaped out of their way and hid in the sage-brush. Prairie dogs whistled warnings and disappeared in their underground burrows, as the horses galloped by.

Chief Curly Bear had been brought to the bunkhouse of the ranch by his friends. The doctor set the broken leg and made his old Indian friend comfortable. He said that the chief would have to remain in bed, where he was, until his leg was better. The Indians from the reservation pulled the wagon out of the gully and went home. Molly Antelope went with them, riding behind Tom White Calf. Ben watched the four braves and Molly until they dropped out of sight in the hollow beyond Rattlesnake Hill. Then he brushed and combed the little appaloosa until his coat shone like silk.

Ben and the old Indian chief became good friends while the broken leg was mending. Curly Bear often spoke of the Great Spirit who ruled the Indian country, long before the white men came. He told Ben of the days when the plains were black with herds of grazing buffalo. Then the elk and antelope were plentiful, too, and there was enough food for all. Ben listened wide-eyed to tales of mighty hunters and great Shoshone chiefs of the past.

When Curly Bear's leg was strong enough for him to be moved, he returned home. But the old Indian never forgot the kindness and help given him by his young friend. Not long after his return to the Reservation, Molly Antelope appeared at the kitchen door of the ranch house with a message for Ben.

"There was a big talk last night," she said. "My grandfather and the other chiefs have made you a son of the Shoshones. Your Indian name is Little Spotted Horse." Molly Antelope stopped talking and with a shy smile slipped away.

"Yippeeee!" shouted Ben. He was proud to have been adopted by the Shoshones. "Hey, Mom," he called. "I'm an Indian. Yippeee!"

Ben's mother was pleased when she heard Molly Antelope's message. She, too, had been adopted by the tribe when she was a little girl. The Indians were her friends.

"That is a great honor," she said. "I hope you will always be a good Indian."

Late that spring, Ben's father and his men brought the big herd of white-faced cattle up from the winter grazing ground. Now, they were getting fat on the rich green grass of the range near the home ranch. The cowboy's camp was in a big hollow just beyond Lookout Hill.

One day, three-fingered Jake, the camp cook, drove into the ranch house yard. He had come for some flour and bacon. Ben

and Pal went back to the camp with him. Ben's father and the cowboys were glad to see them. The spring roundup was a busy time and they needed extra help.

Ben and his pony liked life on the open range. They helped round up the stray cattle at night. They watched the cowboys at work and learned to separate calves from the herd, and Ben learned how to rope and tie them for branding.

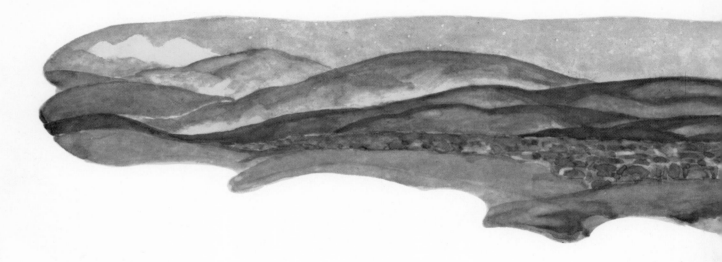

After the day's work was done and supper eaten, the cowboys gathered around an open fire near the cook wagon. While
Wyoming Wally strummed his guitar, they sang songs of the
range, or listened to the old-timers spin tales of stampeding
Texas longhorns, horse thieves and fights with grizzly bears.
And they talked a lot about the big celebration to be held in town
on the Fourth of July. Everyone was going to the rodeo, some
to try to ride the bucking horses, some to show their skill at
roping calves. All were sure they would win a prize. Ben was
thrilled by the cowboys' talk. When he felt sleepy, he rolled up
in his blanket and pillowed his head on his saddle. Then he gazed
at the twinkling stars in the wide, dark sky overhead, until he
fell asleep to dream of the rodeo and the cheering crowds. His
pony grazed contentedly nearby.

Cowboys came from far and near to take part in the Fourth of July rodeo. Ben on the appaloosa and his father on the big black horse, rode in the parade. Chief Curly Bear and Molly Antelope, as well as many other Indians from the reservation, were in the parade, too. The broad main street of the town was gay with flags and banners. Horses and horsemen were everywhere.

After the parade, the townspeople and visitors went to the big field next to the Indian camp to see the rodeo.

Everyone enjoyed the excitement of the horse races and cheered the lucky riders who stayed on the bucking horses.

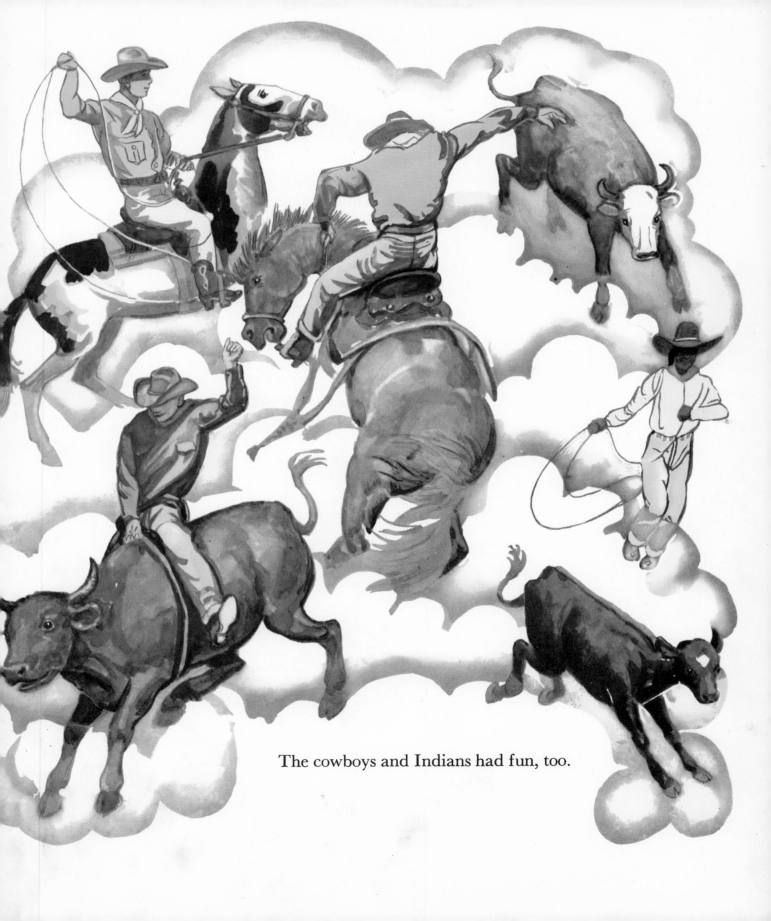

The cowboys and Indians had fun, too.

When the calf-roping contest was called, Ben slipped quietly out of the crowd and hurried to get his pony. Then he took his place with the cowboys waiting their turn at the chute just south of the grandstand. He hadn't told his father or mother that he had entered the contest. He wanted to surprise them.

Texas Pete made fast time with the first calf and the crowd cheered loudly. The next calf dodged the lasso and Arizona Joe was out of the contest. One after the other, the cowboys roped and tied the calves. Then Ben's turn came. A black calf galloped into the field before the grandstand. The barrier in front of the chute dropped. Ben swung his lasso. The loop circled above his pony's head. "Go get him, Pal," he said. The spotted pony left the chute like a rocket. Ben made a perfect throw and caught his calf. "Hold him, Pal," he shouted. The appaloosa stopped in his tracks . . . And so did the calf. Ben leaped from the saddle.

He knew his pony would keep the lasso taut. He ran to the calf, tumbled him to the ground, and before you could say "Jack Robinson," had tied three of the calf's legs. He waved his hands above his head to let the judges know he had tied his calf, just as he had seen the other ropers do.

When the judge's flag went down, Ben removed his lasso and untied the calf. Breathless and with pounding heart he waited to hear what the judges would say. A great burst of hand-clapping and cheers swept the grandstand, when the roping time was called out. Ben and his spotted pony had broken the record. He was the new calf-roping champion. Ben was so surprised he couldn't talk but he was very happy. So were his father and mother, who cheered from the grandstand.

A stranger in town had seen the wonderful performance of young Ben and the spotted pony. He didn't wait to watch the cowboys rope and ride the wild horses from the range. He left his seat in the grandstand and was waiting by the hitching rail, when Ben rode up. The stranger owned a dude ranch up in the Jackson Hole country. He was starting a herd of appaloosas and he wanted very much the spotted pony he had just seen. He was a man of few words.

"I'll give a thousand dollars for that pony, my boy," he said. "Who owns him?" His keen eyes took in all the fine points of the beautiful young horse.

Ben was too surprised to answer right away. He tied Pal to the rail and stared at the stranger. He had never thought of selling his pony, but a thousand dollars seemed like an awful lot of money. He thought of some of the things he could buy with all that money. There was that fine guitar in the music store. It could be his if he sold the pony. And he could buy the silver-mounted saddle his father had looked at in the saddler's shop. He could have a new hat, shirts, and boots, and the mail order catalogue at home was full of pretty things he could buy

for his mother. Then he looked at his pony and the little appaloosa looked at him. Pictures of happy hours in the saddle flashed before his eyes. Ben remembered the long rides to and from the ranch school and the fun they had at the roundup. And he thought of the day his sturdy little pony had brought him safely home when he was lost in the blizzard. And only a few minutes ago, the spotted pony had helped him win the calf-roping championship. He turned to the stranger.

"He's MY pony, sir," he said. "I couldn't sell him, we're PALS."

The little spotted pony shook his mane, stamped his feet, and neighed loudly. Ben was sure he understood.

The stranger was disappointed but he was a real horseman. He patted Ben on the back.

"You couldn't have a better pal," he said. "He is a wonderful little appaloosa."

BOOKS BY

Berta and Elmer Hader

THE FARMER IN THE DELL

COCK-A-DOODLE-DOO

PANCHO

THE MIGHTY HUNTER

THE LITTLE STONE HOUSE

BIG CITY

THE BIG SNOW

LOST IN THE ZOO

LITTLE WHITEFOOT

THE FRIENDLY PHOEBE

THE RUNAWAYS

DING DONG BELL

LITTLE CHIP

REINDEER TRAIL

MR. BILLY'S GUN

QUACK-QUACK

LITTLE ANTELOPE

SNOW IN THE CITY

TWO IS COMPANY, THREE'S A CROWD

LITTLE APPALOOSA